This book belongs to

....

Also by Tony Hickey

Mouse and the Lemon Boy

Tony Hickey

Mouse and the Lemon Boy

Illustrated by Kate Walsh

Children's
POOLBEG

First published 1993 by
Poolbeg,
A Division of Poolbeg Enterprises Ltd,
Knocksedan House,
Swords, Co Dublin, Ireland.

© Tony Hickey 1993

The moral right of the author has been asserted.

A catalogue record for this book is available from the British Library.

ISBN 1 85371 273 6

Illustrated by Kate Walsh
Cover design by Poolbeg
Set by Mac Book Limited in Stone 9/13
Printed by The Guernsey Press Company,
Vale, Guernsey, Channel Islands.

*To Lucy and Alan and All Ducks Who
Dance*

Contents

Contents

1

The Shop Window

Mouse and the Lemon Boy lived in the middle of a shop window. Mouse was made of marshmallow and was a pretty pink colour.

The Lemon Boy was made of lemon candy and was a bright yellow colour.

For a while, they were both very happy living in the middle of the shop window. The shop was on a busy street and near to a school. Lots of children and grown-ups looked in at them every day.

Some of the children would say, "Oh, look at the lovely mouse! Oh, look at the lovely lemon boy! I am going to save up and buy both of them!"

But no one ever did buy them. This was because the children got their pocket

money on Fridays after school was over. But none of them lived near the shop, so by the time they came back to school on Monday morning, they had spent all their pocket money.

Then they would say, "Oh dear, we forgot about buying the mouse and the lemon boy when we got our pocket money this week. We will make a special journey back to the shop to buy them!"

But, of course, none of the children ever did remember, and when Monday came around again, the children would say the very same thing. And so it went on and on and on until one Sunday morning the Lemon Boy said, "I am fed up!"

Mouse said, "What do you mean, you are fed up?"

"Well, another Saturday has come and gone and none of the children remembered to come and buy us. Today is Sunday. The shop doesn't open on Sunday so no one can buy us today. Tomorrow is Monday. I'll bet you anything you like that, when the children pass on their way to school,

3

they will say the same thing as they always do. They will say, 'Oh, dear, we forgot to buy the mouse and the lemon boy when we got our pocket money! Still, never mind, we will try and remember when we get our pocket money this week. We will make a special journey back here to the shop to buy them.' But they never do remember!"

"Well, I don't see what we can do about that," said Mouse. "We can't force them to remember. And we are luckier than some of the things in this shop window. Some of them have been here much longer than we have!"

"That's true," said a plastic spider who lived in a dusty corner of the window. "I've been here for a long, long time without anyone wanting to buy me."

"That may be true," said the Lemon Boy, "but I don't want to be here a long, long time! I want to get out of this shop window! I want to see the big world!"

"Then why don't you go and look at it?" said Mouse. "You have legs, which is more than I have."

"I'm not sure that I can move my legs," said the Lemon Boy.

"Why don't you try?" asked Mouse.

The Lemon Boy tried but his legs didn't move. He sighed and said, "It's no good. They don't move. But are you sure you don't have legs?"

"Oh, yes," said Mouse. "I am quite sure. I am flat underneath. The people who made me didn't think that I needed legs."

"Perhaps you could just slide along the ground," a gentle voice said.

Mouse and the Lemon Boy looked all around them but could not see who had spoken.

"I am up here on the top shelf," the same gentle voice said.

Mouse and the Lemon Boy, and everything else in the window, looked up at the top shelf. There, standing on the edge of the shelf, was a Christmas tree fairy.

"Who are you?" asked the Lemon Boy.

"I am the Christmas tree fairy," replied

the tiny little figure. "My name is Twinkle. The man who owns the shop put me up on this shelf when he took the Christmas tree down last year. I think he has forgotten all about me."

"I think he has forgotten all about all of us," said the Lemon Boy.

"Now, now," said Twinkle. "You must never say that. Things can always get better. Maybe I can help you."

"How can you do that?" asked Mouse.

"Do you see this wand that I have in my hand?" Twinkle waved the wand, which was the colour of silver with a gold star on the top.

"Yes, we see it," said Mouse and the Lemon Boy.

"Well, it is just possible that, if you really want something, this wand will make your wish come true," said Twinkle. "Now, Lemon Boy, do you really want to be able to go for a walk and see the big world?"

"Yes," said the Lemon Boy. "I really do want to be able to do that."

"And, Mouse, what about you?" asked

6

Twinkle. "Do you really want to be able to slide along the ground beside the Lemon Boy?"

Mouse thought for a second. Then she said, "Yes, I do."

"Very well," said Twinkle. "Let me wave my wand over the two of you."

Twinkle flew down off the shelf and waved her hand.

A shower of moonbeams fell from the wand and landed on Mouse and the Lemon Boy.

Everything in the shop waited to see what might happen next.

Then the Lemon Boy lifted his left arm. Then he lifted his right arm.

The he lifted his left leg. Then he lifted his right leg.

Then he sat up.

Then he stood up.

Then he walked all around the shop window. "I can walk!" he said. "I can walk! I can walk! I can walk!"

"Hurrah! Hurrah!" went everything in the shop.

Then the plastic spider said, "All right, Mouse, see if you can move!"

Mouse gave herself a little push and slid a short distance. Then she gave a bigger push and Whoosh! she slid all the way across the window and landed on the shop counter.

Then she slid all the way along the counter as far as the cash register. "Hurrah! Hurrah!" she squeaked. "It worked! Twinkle's magic wand works! I can slide just as well as if I had legs. Oh, but why don't all of you come for a walk with the Lemon Boy and me?"

"Yes, do," said the Lemon Boy. "It's a lovely day for a walk!"

"I'm not sure that is a good idea," said Twinkle.

"Oh, and why not?" asked the Lemon Boy.

"You might attract too much attention if you all went for a walk at the same time," said Twinkle. "So why don't you and Mouse set off now? When you come back you can tell us all your adventures."

"All right," said the Lemon Boy.

The Lemon Boy stepped carefully down onto the counter next to Mouse. Then he climbed carefully off the counter down onto the floor.

Mouse leaned over the edge of the counter and looked down at him. "Oh dear," Mouse said. "I'm not sure that I can get all the way down there. It looks like a long, long way."

"Jump!" said the Lemon Boy. "You are made of marshmallow so you are not very heavy. I'm sure that I will be able to catch you."

"Yes, of course, he will be able to catch you," everything in the shop yelled, except, of course, Twinkle.

She was too quiet to yell. Instead, she gave her wand just the tiniest wave that not even Mouse noticed. A few moonbeams landed on Mouse's head.

Suddenly Mouse felt very brave. She jumped right off the edge of the counter. The Lemon Boy caught her and put her down on the ground.

"Hurrah! Hurrah!" everything in the shop yelled again. "Mouse and the Lemon Boy are going for a walk, are going for a walk!"

A brass band of toy monkeys began to play loud marching music. Everything in the shop began to sing,

Oh Mouse is going for a walk
For a walk
For a walk
Oh Mouse is going for a walk
At six o'clock in the morning.

"Don't forget that I am going as well," said the Lemon Boy. "Don't forget that it was all my idea!"

"Of course we won't," said Twinkle. She began to sing,

The Lemon Boy is going out
Is going out
Is going out
The Lemon Boy is going out
At six o'clock in the morning.

Everything in the shop joined in with Twinkle's song.

Then they all sang the song about Mouse again.

"Oh, isn't all this wonderful!" said Mouse. "But how do we get out of the shop onto the street?"

"That's easy," said the Lemon Boy. "We use the letter box."

The letter box in the front door was down at the bottom of the door.

The Lemon Boy held it open and pushed Mouse through it. Then he managed to scramble through as well.

"Well, well," he said, "so here we are, out of the shop at long last!"

"Yes," said Mouse, waving her whiskers at all the toys who had crowded into the window to look at them. "Which way are we going to go?"

"This way," said the Lemon Boy, for no reason at all except that he felt like saying it. Off he walked down the street with Mouse sliding along beside him.

2

The Park

The street was very quiet.

There were no people, no cars and no buses.

"It's as quiet out here as it was in the shop window," said the Lemon Boy.

"That is because it is Sunday," said Mouse. "The offices and the shops do not open on Sunday. The schools are closed as well. It is also early in the morning."

"Yes, but if there are no people or children here, everything in the shop could have come for a walk with us. No one would have even seen us," said the Lemon Boy.

"I think Twinkle was just being nice when she said that just you and I should go for a walk," answered Mouse. "I think she knew that the other things in the shop were afraid to leave the shop."

"In other words, you and I are the bravest things in the shop," said the Lemon Boy.

"Yes, I suppose you could say that," said Mouse.

To be one of the two bravest things in the shop made the Lemon Boy feel much happier. He no longer minded the street being so quiet. He walked along humming the song that Twinkle had made up.

Mouse slid along beside him. She looked at the tall office buildings and the big clothes shops and the lovely bookshops. "I never knew the big world could be as big as this," she said.

"Neither did I," said the Lemon Boy.

Then he and Mouse stopped and stared at a big, wide piece of grass with high railings around it. There were beautiful trees and lovely flowers growing there.

The flowers were all different colours. There were red flowers and blue flowers. There were green flowers and purple flowers.

There were pink flowers, the same colour as Mouse.

There were yellow flowers, the same colour as the Lemon Boy.

"I wonder what this place is," said Mouse.

"I don't know," said the Lemon Boy. "But I think we should go and have a look at it."

Together, Mouse and the Lemon Boy went in through the open gate, then along a grey path. They had not gone far when they heard a very strange sound.

"What is that?" asked the Lemon Boy.

"I don't know," said Mouse. "But it is coming from over there." Mouse and the Lemon Boy hurried along the path to the top of a small hill.

They saw a big flat space. At first, they thought it was a huge looking-glass like the one that was in the shop.

Then the glass became all wavy as a group of beautiful creatures came out of the bushes and sat on top of the glass.

"What kind of glass can this be?" asked the Lemon Boy.

"It isn't glass. It's water," said Mouse. "It is the way that the beautiful creatures move that makes the water go wavy. And it is the way they speak to each other that makes the strange sound. Just listen!"

"Quack," went the beautiful creatures. "Quack, quack, quack, quack!"

"I wonder what they can be?" said Mouse.

"Ducks! We are ducks," a ducky sort of voice said.

Mouse and the Lemon Boy looked around.

A little fat duck was waddling down the path towards them. She said, "I am a duck. My friends on the lake are ducks. I've been for a walk in search of bread."

"We are on a walk too," said Mouse.

"That's right," said the Lemon Boy. "We want to see the great big world."

"Well, you have come to the right place," said the duck. "This is the centre of the world!"

"Is it?" said the Lemon Boy. "Is it *really* the centre of the world?"

"It is as far as ducks are concerned," said the duck. "What are your names?"

"I'm Mouse," said Mouse.

"I'm the Lemon Boy," said the Lemon Boy. "Who are you?"

"I am Waddle," said the duck.

"And does this place have a name apart from being the centre of the world for ducks?" asked Mouse.

"It certainly does," said Waddle. "It is called 'the park'. Humans come and sit here on warm days and look at the flowers. Children come and play games here. Sometimes dogs come in as well. They are supposed to be on leads. But sometimes they are not. They bark and bark at us. They even come into the water and try to catch us."

"And do they catch you?" asked Mouse

"Of course not," said Waddle. "Ducks are too clever to be caught. Everyone knows that. But then maybe the two of you are not as clever as everyone else."

"I'm sure that we are," said the Lemon Boy, feeling cross at what Waddle had said.

"Well, you didn't know that this was the park. You didn't know that that was a lake. Now that I come to think of it, you didn't even know that ducks were ducks," said Waddle.

"That is because there were no ducks in the shop window to tell us about these things," said Mouse.

"Ducks in a shop window!" said Waddle in amazement. "What are you talking about?"

Mouse and the Lemon Boy told Waddle the story of how they had been living in the middle of the shop window and how Twinkle had waved her wand so that they could go for a walk.

"That is a very interesting story indeed," said Waddle. "I think you should tell it again to all my friends."

Waddle rushed down to the edge of the lake and called out, "Quacko, quacko! I've just heard a very interesting story. You had better come out of the water if you want to hear it too."

Now there was nothing that ducks liked

better than an interesting story, especially on a quiet Sunday morning in the park.

"We will be right there," they said.

They stopped swimming around and came out of the lake.

They made a huge circle around Mouse and the Lemon Boy.

Mouse and the Lemon Boy once more told their story of getting out of the shop window.

"Amazing!" the ducks said. "Really amazing!"

"Exactly," said Waddle. "But now that they have told us their story, we must do something for them."

"Would they like to come swimming?" asked one of the other ducks.

"I don't think water would be a very good idea," said Mouse. "I'd go all gungey. The Lemon Boy might melt."

"We could take you flying around the park," said another duck. "Would you like that?"

"Oh, yes," said the Lemon Boy. "We would love to do that."

The two best flying ducks, named Feather and Beak, fluffed up their wings. Mouse slid onto Feather's back. The Lemon Boy climbed onto Beak's back.

"Okay. Off we go!" said Beak.

And off they went, straight up into the air and all around the park.

Mouse and the Lemon Boy could see all the trees and all the flowers and the lake and the ducks all at the same time.

Feather and Beak flew down out of the air and landed back at the lake.

"That was wonderful," said Mouse.

"Yes, it was," said the Lemon Boy.

"Good," said Waddle. "Now we are going to dance the duck dance for you. In fact you could probably learn it yourselves. It is very easy!"

"I can't dance," said Mouse.

"You can slide around in time to the music," said the Lemon Boy. "But I don't see the band."

"We don't need a band," said Waddle. "We make our own music. Now just listen and watch."

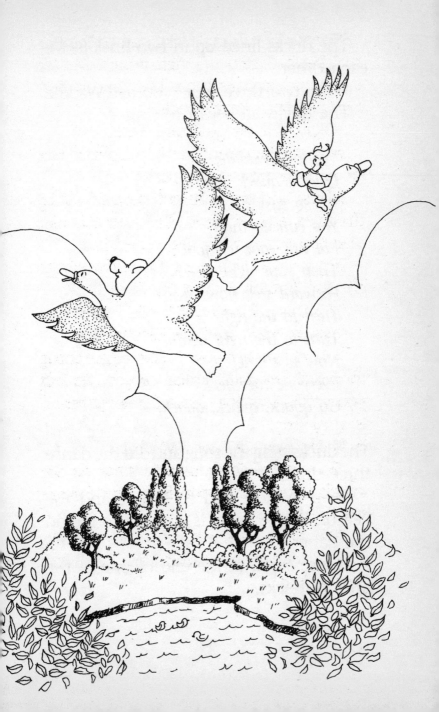

The ducks lined up in two lines facing each other.

"One, two, three, four," counted Waddle.

The ducks all began to sing.

Waddle, waddle,
Quack, quack, quack.
It's so easy
You can do that!
Put out your left foot
Then your right
Forward step now
Turn to the right
Turn to the right again
Now to the left
Everyone together
Go quack, quack, quack.

The ducks sang the song and did the dance three times.

Then Waddle said to Mouse and the Lemon Boy, "Now it is time for you to do the dance."

Mouse stood at the end of one of the lines of ducks.

The Lemon Boy stood at the end of the other line.

"One, two, three," counted Waddle.

They all sang as loud as they could and danced as well as they could. It was so easy that Mouse had no trouble sliding along to the music. She was delighted when they did the dance a second time.

They were going to do it a third time when they heard the sound of human voices.

"It's those boys," Waddle said crossly.

"What boys?" asked the Lemon Boy.

"Those boys over there." Waddle pointed with one of her wings in the direction of the park gates.

Mouse and the Lemon Boy could see the heads of four boys just above the top of the hill. The boys' heads kept bobbing up and down.

"Are they doing a dance as well?" asked Mouse.

"No," said Waddle. "They are on skateboards. They are not supposed to bring them into the park."

"Then why did they bring them into the park?" asked the Lemon Boy.

"Because they know there will be no one here so early on a Sunday morning," said Beak.

"No one, that is, except us ducks," said Feather.

"They sometimes try to run over us," said Waddle crossly. "In fact, here they come now."

The four boys on their skate-boards had zoomed along the path and were now looking down at the ducks.

"You ducks had better get out of the way!" the biggest boy yelled. Then he and the three other boys came rushing down the path towards the pond.

The ducks quacked angrily as they rushed out into the middle of the lake.

Mouse and the Lemon Boy ran and hid under a bush.

But they were not quick enough. One of the boys had seen them.

He said to the other boys, "Did you see what I saw?"

"No," said the other boys. "What did you see?"

"I saw something pink and something yellow run under that bush," the boy said. "They are the strangest things I've ever seen."

"Maybe they came from a flying saucer," said the biggest of the boys. "If we caught them we could become famous."

The four boys bent down and began to look under the bush.

Mouse and the Lemon Boy stood as still as they could.

"I can't see anything," the big boy said. "We need a stick to poke around with."

"There's a stick over here," the first boy said.

All the boys turned and looked at where he was pointing.

The Lemon Boy picked up Mouse and carried her from under the bush to where some of the pink flowers were growing. He pushed her under them. "Stay here," he said.

Then he hid under a bunch of yellow

flowers.

The big boy ran and got the stick. The others watched as he poked about under the bush. They hadn't seen Mouse and the Lemon Boy getting away.

"There's nothing here," the big boy said.

"Maybe they are hiding under a different bush," said the second boy. "Let's look under this one here."

The boys moved away from where Mouse and the Lemon Boy were hiding.

The Lemon Boy ran over to the pink flowers and whispered to Mouse, "Come on. We might be able to get out of the park now without being seen."

"All right," said Mouse. "But you don't need to carry me. I can slide very easily across the grass."

"All right," said the Lemon Boy.

Together they hurried across the grass. When they reached a big rose tree they stopped and looked back.

The four boys were now looking under different bushes.

"We have no time to waste," said Mouse.

"They could come up here in a few minutes and see us. We must get out of the park."

"You are right," said the Lemon Boy.

"There is the gate," said Mouse

She and the Lemon Boy rushed to the gate and out of the park.

"That was a real adventure," said the Lemon Boy.

"Yes," said Mouse. "But maybe now we should go back to the shop. It is down this way."

But Mouse was wrong.

The shop was not where she was pointing.

The shop was not in that street at all.

Mouse and the Lemon Boy had come out of the park by a different gate from the one they had come in by.

But they had been so busy getting away from the boys on the skate-boards that they did not notice.

Instead of going back to the shop, Mouse and the Lemon Boy were going further and further away from it.

3

The Merry-go-round

Mouse and the Lemon Boy had gone down the wrong street for five minutes when the Lemon Boy said, "I don't think the shop was this far away from the park!"

Mouse said, "You don't think we are lost, do you? I wish there was someone we could ask. I suppose we will just have to wait here until someone nice and friendly comes by."

But the Lemon Boy did not answer Mouse. He was not even listening to her. He had even forgotten all about being lost and chased and being in the wrong street. Instead, he was staring at something even more amazing than the park and the ducks.

What he saw looked like a circle of horses.

"Is that a circle of horses?" he asked Mouse.

"Yes," said Mouse, "but they don't look a bit like the horse that we sometimes see going past the shop window."*

The horse that Mouse and the Lemon Boy saw going past the shop window belonged to Mr Murphy.

Mr Murphy collected bits of iron and old furniture that no one wanted.

His horse's name was Mac. Mac pulled the cart into which Mr Murphy put the bits of iron and old furniture.

"You are right," said the Lemon Boy. "These horses do look very different from old Mac. They are all different colours."

"And their feet don't touch the ground," said Mouse. "How can they stand up if their feet don't touch the ground?"

"Let's go and ask them," said the Lemon Boy.

"All right," said Mouse. "They might also tell us how to get back to the shop."

Mouse and the Lemon Boy walked up to the circle of horses and said, "Excuse us.

31

Can you help us? We are lost!"

"Lost?" said a horse with a yellow mane. "How can you be lost?"

"We can't find the shop where we live," said Mouse.

"You live in a shop?" said the horse with the yellow mane.

"Well, actually it is in the window of the shop," said the Lemon Boy.

"You live in the window of a shop?" said the horse with the yellow mane. "I've never heard of such a thing."

"Neither have we," said all the other horses.

"And we have never heard of horses who could stand without their feet touching the ground," said the Lemon Boy. "Why do you not fall over?"

"We do not fall over because we are not ordinary horses," said the horse with the yellow mane.

"What kind are you then?" asked Mouse.

"We are merry-go-round horses," said the horse with the yellow mane. "We go up and down and all around in a circle.

People come from miles around and pay to sit on our backs."

"How wonderful," said Mouse. "But if you are not real horses, what are you made of?"

"We are made of wood," said the horse with the yellow mane. "What are the two of you made of?"

"I'm made of pink marshmallow," said Mouse.

"And I am made of lemon sugar candy," said the Lemon Boy.

"Oh, I see," said the horse with the yellow mane. "That is why the two of you live in a shop window. You are hoping that someone might buy you."

"Yes," said Mouse. "That is our wish."

"I have another wish as well," said the Lemon Boy. "I wish that I could go for a ride on the merry-go-round."

"We don't have any money to pay," said Mouse.

"And the man who makes the merry-go-round go round isn't here," said the horse with the yellow mane.

"So my wish will never come true," said the Lemon Boy.

He looked so sad that the horse with the yellow mane said, "Wait a second."

He turned and began to whisper to the other horses.

They whispered back.

Then they all nodded their heads.

The horse with the yellow mane said, "We could start the merry-go-round ourselves. We just have to press that button over there. We have never started the merry-go-round by ourselves before. We are going to do it now because you are lost and because the Lemon Boy looks so sad."

"You are very kind," said Mouse.

"Pick a pony," said the horse with the yellow mane. "That's what the man who makes the roundabout go always says before he makes it go round."

"I'll pick you, if that's all right," said Mouse.

"Of course it is all right," said the horse with the yellow mane.

"I will help you up," said the Lemon

Boy.

He very gently lifted Mouse onto the horse with the yellow mane.

"Snuggle into my mane," said the horse. "That way you won't fall off."

It was now the Lemon Boy's turn to pick a pony.

"I would like to ride around on that wonderful blue horse," he said.

He hurried to the blue horse and climbed up on its back.

"Are we all ready then?" asked the horse with the yellow mane.

"Yes," shouted all the other horses.

"Good," said the horse with the yellow mane. It leaned forwards and touched the button with its left ear.

The merry-go-round began to go around.

At first it went very slowly.

Then it began to go faster and faster.

Lovely music began to play.

The horses began to sing the merry-go-round song.

Here we go round the merry-go-round
The merry-go-round
The merry-go-round
Here we go round the merry-go-round
At eight o'clock in the morning.

The song was very like the one that the toys in the shop had sung. Mouse and the Lemon Boy didn't mind this at all. They were having a lovely time, for not only did the merry-go-round go around and around but the horses went up and down in the air at the same time.

They sang the second verse of their song.

Here we go
All up in the air
All up in the air
All up in the air
Then we all go
Down in the air
At eight o'clock in the morning.

Then the horses all went "Neigh! Neigh!

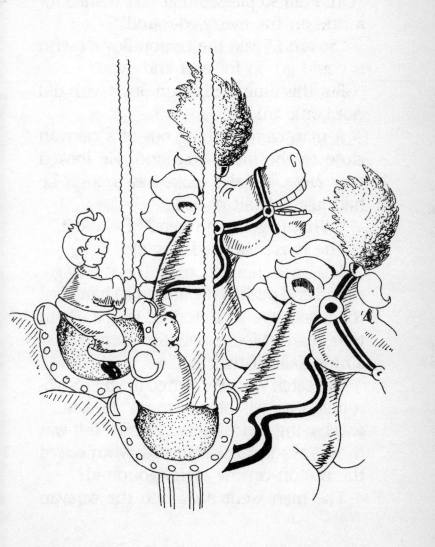

Neigh!" and flicked their tails.

Mouse called out to the Lemon Boy, "Oh, I am so pleased that you wished for a ride on the merry-go-round!"

"So am I," said the Lemon Boy. "I wish it could go on for ever and ever!"

But this time the Lemon Boy's wish did not come true.

A man came rushing out of a caravan close to the merry-go-round. He looked very cross. He also looked as though he had just got out of bed.

"What is going on here?" he asked.

The horses stopped singing.

The man jumped onto the merry-go-round and pushed the button so hard that the merry-go-round stopped with a wham that made Mouse and the Lemon Boy almost fall off their horses.

"If I catch whoever started the merry-go-round, they will be very sorry!" he said. "I was having a nice lie-in. I wonder if it was those boys on the skate-boards who pressed the button on the merry-go-round?"

The man went back into the caravan

and shut the door.

Mouse said to the Lemon Boy, "We must get away from here as quickly as possible."

He jumped down off the blue horse and helped Mouse down off the horse with the yellow mane.

"Thank you very much," Mouse said to all the horses.

But the horses made no sound back.

"They are afraid that the man in the caravan might hear them if they speak," said the Lemon Boy. "Come on quickly!"

Mouse and the Lemon Boy hurried away from the merry-go-round.

They did not slow down until they were around the next corner.

Then Mouse said, "Oh dear, we forgot to ask the horses the way back to the shop."

"We can't go back and ask now," said the Lemon Boy. "The cross man in the caravan might catch us. We will have to go further along this street and see what happens."

4

The Fishing Boat

Mouse and the Lemon Boy had not gone far along the street when they came to a bridge.

The bridge went across a river. Mouse said, "I don't think we should go across this bridge."

"But it's a lovely bridge," said the Lemon Boy.

"I know that," said Mouse. "But I don't think it will bring us back to our shop."

The Lemon Boy was no longer listening to Mouse. Instead he was looking down through the pillars of the bridge at a lovely fishing boat that was sailing down the river.

"Oh, look at the lovely boat," he said. "Isn't it just like the toy one that's on the second shelf of our shop?"

Mouse looked down at the fishing boat. "You are right," Mouse said. "It *does* look like the toy boat on the second shelf of our shop. Of course the fishing boat on the river is much bigger."

"That is because the fishing boat on the river is a real boat," said the Lemon Boy.

"Yes, I know that," said Mouse. She leaned forward to get a better look at the boat. There was a gust of wind that blew her into the air. She called out, "Oh dear! Help! Help!"

The Lemon Boy tried to catch her.

There was a second gust of wind.

This time the Lemon Boy was blown up into the air.

He and Mouse looked at each other. They were very frightened. Then they began to fall down, down towards the river.

"If we land in the river, I will go all gungey," said Mouse.

"And I will probably melt!" said the Lemon Boy.

But they did not land in the river. Instead, they landed on the deck of the fishing

boat, which just happened to be underneath them at that moment!

"Oh, how lucky we were that the fishing boat was underneath us at that moment," said the Lemon Boy.

"Yes, we were very lucky," said Mouse.

Then a voice said, "Who are you?"

Mouse and the Lemon Boy looked up. They saw a boy and a girl looking down at them.

"Please," said Mouse, "we are Mouse and the Lemon Boy."

"And how did you get on this fishing boat?" asked the boy.

"The wind blew us off the bridge," said the Lemon Boy.

"And what were you doing on the bridge?" asked the girl.

"We were trying to find our way back to the shop where we live," said Mouse.

"Is that the shop near the school?" asked the boy.

"Yes," said the Lemon Boy. Now that he was safe on the boat, he no longer felt frightened.

Mouse did not feel frightened either. She said, "I think I have seen the two of you before. I think you come and look in the window of the shop."

"That's right," said the girl.

"What are your names?" asked Mouse

"My name is Nan," said the girl.

"And mine is Sam," said the boy. "Nan is my sister."

"And Sam is my brother," said Nan. "We often thought it might be nice to buy the two of you."

"Lots of children say that," said the Lemon Boy. "But they never come back when they get their pocket money. What are the two of you doing on this fishing boat?"

"It belongs to our father," said Sam. "The engine was broken. We had to have it fixed at a special place back down the river."

"Now we are going fishing in the sea," said Nan.

"What is the sea?" asked Mouse.

"It is a place made of water," said Sam.

"I hope we won't get wet," said Mouse.

"Of course you won't get wet," said Nan. "We have been on the boat for hours and hours. We aren't wet."

"What makes the boat go?" asked the Lemon Boy.

"The engine," said Nan. "Our dad is in the cabin steering the boat."

She pointed to what looked like a tiny little house at the back of the boat. It had a window. Through the window Mouse and the Lemon Boy could see a man steering the boat. He had a very kind face.

"I hope he won't mind us being on the boat," said Mouse.

"It might be best if he didn't see you," said Sam. "The boat is going to take you a long, long way from the shop."

"Oh dear, oh dear!" said Mouse. "Twinkle will be very worried."

"Who is Twinkle?" asked Sam.

"She is the fairy who did the magic," said Mouse.

"Oh, please tell us the whole story," said Nan.

"All right," said Mouse.

Mouse and the Lemon Boy told Nan and Sam all the things that had happened to them since they had left the shop.

"You have had a lot of adventures," said Nan.

"Yes," said Mouse. "But now we would like to go back to the shop."

"Oh, but first we have to see the sea," said the Lemon Boy. "We might never get the chance again."

"We could take you back to the shop later on," said Nan.

"Yes, of course we could," said Sam. "Now come and sit on this pile of ropes. You can see everything much better from here."

Nan and Sam lifted Mouse and the Lemon Boy on top of a pile of ropes.

Mouse and the Lemon Boy looked at all the things there were to be seen.

First, they saw big ships, tied up along the river.

"Those ships come from all over the world," said Sam. "When I grow up I am going to travel all over the world. I am going to see all the places that those ships come from."

"So am I," said Nan.

"Will you go on the fishing boat?" asked Mouse.

"No. This fishing boat is too small to go to those faraway places," said Nan. "We might go in a big boat."

"Or in an aeroplane," said Sam.

"There was an aeroplane in the shop," said Mouse. "Someone bought it to give it to someone else as a birthday present."

"The aeroplane that we are talking about would be much bigger than that," said Sam.

"It would be as big as that one up there in the sky," said Nan.

Mouse and the Lemon Boy looked up at the sky. They saw an aeroplane way, way up very high. The sun was shining on it.

"It looks like a big silver bird," said Mouse.

A seagull, who was flying past, heard what Mouse had said. It came and perched on the boat. "Would you like to go and have a closer look at the aeroplane?" asked the seagull.

"You could never fly that high in the sky," said the Lemon Boy.

"Of course I could," said the seagull. The seagull flapped its wings and began to sing a very strange song.

Seagulls fly high in the sky
High in the sky
High in the sky
Where they eat fresh blackberry pie
And count fish.

"That is the strangest song I have ever heard," said Sam.

"Is it really?" said the seagull. "I made it up myself."

"With some help from all of us," said a group of seagulls that had perched on the roof of the cabin of the boat.

"Would you like to hear the rest of the song?" they all asked.

"Yes, we would," said Mouse and the Lemon Boy and the two children.

"Good," said the seagulls.

They all flew into the air and began to sing.

Seagulls fly high in the sky
High in the sky
High in the sky
Where they eat fresh strawberry pie
And count fish.

Then they all flapped their wings and called out, "Gulls! Gulls! We are singing seagulls and this is our song!"

"It's a very nice song," said Mouse. "Thank you for singing it for us."

"Oh, but it's not finished yet," said the first seagull.

All the seagulls began to sing again.

Seagulls fly high in the sky
High in the sky
High in the sky
Where they eat fresh baked apple pie
And count fish.

"Wait a second," said Sam. "All the words

are the same except for the kind of pie you eat high in the sky."

"That's right," said the seagull. "That is so that we can all say which kind of pie we like best. What kind of pie do you like best?"

"Fresh pineapple pie," said Sam.

"Then you must sing the song for us now," said the seagull.

Sam sang,

Seagulls fly high in the sky
High in the sky
High in the sky
Where they eat fresh pineapple pie
And count fish.

"Now it is Nan's turn," said the seagull.
Nan sang,

Seagulls fly high in the sky
High in the sky
High in the sky
Where they eat fresh raspberry pie
And count fish.

51

"Now it is the mouse's turn," said the seagull.

"I don't eat pie," said Mouse.

"You don't eat pie!" shouted the seagulls. "We never heard of anything so silly."

"And I never heard anything so silly as your song," said the Lemon Boy. "How can you eat pie in the sky? How can you count fish in the sky?"

"The Lemon Boy is right," said Nan. "Seagulls eat fish. They don't count them."

"What is going on out here?" asked the children's dad. He had heard all the noise and come out of the cabin.

Mouse and the Lemon Boy hid in the ropes.

"The seagulls were teaching us a song," said Nan.

Dad laughed. "Oh, is that so? And I suppose the fish were teaching you a dance?"

"I didn't know fish could dance," said Sam.

Dad laughed again. "Why don't you look into the water and see?" he said. Then he looked at the seagulls and said, "Shoo! Shoo! Go away! You are too noisy!"

The seagulls were very cross with Dad. All the same they did fly away.

Dad went back into the cabin of the fishing boat.

Mouse and the Lemon Boy came out of hiding.

Nan and Sam and Mouse and the Lemon Boy looked over the side of the boat at the water. The water was nice and clear. They could see some very small fish swimming around.

The fish went first to the left. Then to the right. Then they gave a little squiggle forward. Then a little squiggle backwards.

"The way that they are swiming *does* look like a dance," said Mouse.

"I think they are singing too," said the Lemon Boy. "Listen!"

They all listened very carefully.

"You are right," Nan said to the Lemon Boy. "They are singing."

The song that the fish were singing went like this in a gurgly sort of way.

We go swish
We go splash
Under the water
Splash! Splash! Splash!

We swim fast
We swim slow
Where are we going?
We don't know.

But we like it
Yes we do
And we hope
That you do too.

First we go to the left
Then to the right again
Splash! Splash! Splash!

"I like that song much better than the song that the seagulls were singing," said the Lemon Boy.

"So do I," said Nan. "Why don't we try singing it?"

Nan and Sam and the Lemon Boy and

Mouse stood in a line and began to sing the song.

Then they began to pretend to swim and dance.

They had a lovely time. While they were doing the song and dance of the fish, the fishing boat went out onto the sea.

Dad called out from the cabin. "We are at the sea now."

Nan lifted up Mouse. Sam lifted up the Lemon Boy.

Mouse and the Lemon Boy gasped in amazement. They had never imagined that there could be so much water in the world. It seemed to go on for ever and for ever.

"I think the sea is lovely," said the Lemon Boy.

"So do I," said Mouse. "I am glad that we are here. I would be even happier if I knew where the shop was."

"Sam and I will take you back there," said Nan. "We have already told you that."

"Oh, yes," said Mouse. "You did tell us that. I just forgot."

Mouse tried to smile but she did not feel very happy as the fishing boat sailed further and further out into the big, wide sea.

5

The Beach

Dad sailed the boat until he came to where there were other fishing boats. He and Nan and Sam said hello to all the people on the other fishing boats.

All the other people said hello back.

Because Dad's boat was smaller than any of the other boats, he had only Nan and Sam to help him.

The Lemon Boy and Mouse watched them put the nets into the water. Then they watched them take the nets full of fish back out of the water. They watched them empty the nets through a door in the middle of the boat.

In a very short time, Dad said, "We have caught enough fish. The boat is full. How would you like to go to the beach for a while? It is too early to go home."

Sam and Nan were delighted. "We would love to go to the beach," they said. "We really would love that."

"Right then. Off we go." He waved goodbye to all the people in the other fishing boats and went back into the cabin. He turned the boat around and sailed it back across the sea.

"What is 'the beach'?" asked the Lemon Boy.

"Oh, it is a lovely sandy place where we can play and swim," said Nan.

"We won't get wet, will we?" asked Mouse.

"No, of course you won't," said Sam.

That made Mouse happier. "What will happen to all the fish that your dad caught?" she asked.

"Dad will sell it," said Nan. "A lot of people like to eat fish. They will drive out to where he ties up the boat to buy the fish from him."

"He sells it to the people who own the fish shops as well," said Sam.

"Here is the beach now," said Nan.

The beach was just like Nan said it would be. It was a lovely sandy place with children playing and grown-ups reading newspapers or making cups of tea.

"Look! There's Mum," said Sam. He waved at a very pretty woman.

She waved back and called, "Hello, Sam. Hello, Nan. I thought you would come here after you had finished fishing. I brought us all a picnic."

"Oh, good," Sam and Nan called back. Then they ran to tell Dad what was happening.

Dad came out of the cabin. He waved to Mum as well. Then he said to Nan and Sam, "Why don't you swim to the beach from here? I will sail the boat to the little harbour around the corner. The boat will be safe there. Then I will walk around and meet the two of you and Mum."

"All right," Sam said.

"What about Mouse and me?" the Lemon Boy whispered. "We can't go swimming. We would get all wet."

"Oh, dear," said Nan. "That's right."

"You could follow Dad," said Sam. "He doesn't walk very fast."

"Yes, so you could," said Nan.

"Why don't we just wait on the boat?" said Mouse to the Lemon Boy.

"Because we might miss another adventure," said the Lemon Boy.

Nan and Sam took off their jeans and T-shirts. They had their swimsuits on under them. They waved to Mouse and the Lemon Boy. Then they carefully climbed over the side of the boat and down into the water. They swam to the beach.

Dad waited until they were beside Mum before he sailed the boat around the corner to the little harbour.

He tied up the boat and began to walk back to the beach.

The Lemon Boy helped Mouse off the boat onto the land. It was not a very easy thing to do. But somehow he did it. Then they set off after Dad.

They had not gone very far when Mouse said, "I can't keep sliding along like this.

I know Nan and Sam said that their dad did not walk very fast, but he is going far too fast for me."

"I'm feeling tired too," said the Lemon Boy. "Maybe we should have a little rest. If we don't turn up with Dad, Sam and Nan are sure to come and look for us."

Mouse and the Lemon Boy went and sat in the shade of a nice green tree.

"We will be able to see Nan and Sam if they come looking for us," said Mouse.

Then she ran and hid at the bottom of the tree.

"What's wrong?" asked the Lemon Boy.

"There's a dog coming," Mouse said.

The Lemon Boy looked down the road. Mouse was right. There was a dog coming along the road. He was a big black dog. He kept sniffing at the ground.

"I think he's looking for something to eat," said Mouse. "He might try to eat us!"

"We will have to run," said the Lemon Boy.

"I am too tired to run," said Mouse. "Anyway, I could never run faster than the dog—even if I had four legs."

"We will have to climb the tree," said the Lemon Boy. He lifted Mouse as high as he could, which was not very high. "Can you climb up from there?" he asked.

"No, I can't," said Mouse.

"Oh, dear," said the Lemon Boy. "The dog sees us!"

The dog came running to the tree.

"Please don't eat us," said the Lemon Boy. "We are just going for a walk."

"It looks to me as though you were trying to climb that tree," said the dog.

"That is because we were afraid you might try and eat us," said Mouse.

"I have had my breakfast already," said the dog. "Anyway, I don't like lemon candy or marshmallow."

"What do you like then?" asked Mouse, sliding down off the tree.

"I like bones," said the dog. He threw back his head and began to sing.

Woof! Woof! Woof!
My name is Spot

And I've got a lot
Of bones hidden in the garden.

I bury them here
I bury them there
Oh yes, I've got bones in the garden.

And if you would like
I'll show you just how
I bury my bones in the garden.

Spot began to dig a big hole with his front paws.

The Lemon Boy and Mouse crept quietly away. Spot didn't even see them going. He was too busy digging the hole.

Mouse and the Lemon Boy had not gone very far when they heard Nan and Sam calling them.

"We are here!" the Lemon Boy called back.

Nan and Sam ran up to them. "Oh, are you all right?" Nan asked. "We were afraid you might have got lost!"

"No, we didn't get lost," said Mouse,

"but we are very tired. When will you take us back to the shop?"

"We don't know," said Sam. "Mum wants us to spend the whole day at the beach."

"We might not be able to take you back to the shop until we go to school in the morning," said Nan.

"Oh, but Mr Nolan, who owns the shop, will open the shop before you go to school," said Mouse. "He will see that we are not in the window. He might be very cross if he finds out that the Lemon Boy and I have gone for a walk."

"Dear, dear, what are we going to do?" said the Lemon Boy.

"I know," said Sam. "You can go back to the shop on the bus."

"Of course you can," said Nan. "There is a bus that goes from the beach to the street where the shop is. It will not be crowded going back into town. No one will see you."

Nan and Sam picked up Mouse and the Lemon Boy and ran down the road to where the bus was.

The driver of the bus was sitting in the sun, reading a newspaper. He did not see Nan and Sam as they put Mouse and the Lemon Boy on the bus.

"Hide under the front seat," said Nan.

"How will we know when to get off?" asked Mouse.

"Oh, you will know all right," said Sam. "We will see you tomorrow."

Mouse and the Lemon Boy hid under the front seat. The driver folded his newspaper and got back into the bus.

Soon the bus was bouncing and rattling its way back into the city.

6

The Bus

Sam and Nan were right when they said the bus would not be crowded. There was no one waiting at any of the stops.

"What will we do if there is no one at the stop on our street?" whispered Mouse to the Lemon Boy.

"We will just have to think of something," said the Lemon Boy.

The bus driver began to whistle. Then he began to sing,

I like to drive my bus
All around the town
I like the hills that go up
And the hills that go down

I like the streets so full of shops

And so crowded every day.
But most of all I love the
Start of a lovely sunny day

I love to drive my bus
All around the town
I help the people get on
And I help them get down

And when they want the bus to stop
It's a very easy thing
For all they have to do is pull
And my bell will ding-a-ling-ling.

Then the driver went "Ding-a-ling" and
made the noise of the horn on his bus
going "Beep beep."

In fact he was making so much noise
that the Lemon Boy had to speak very
loudly so that Mouse could hear. "All we
have to do to stop the bus is to ring the
bell," he said.

"The bell is far too high up for us to
reach it," said Mouse.

"Maybe we could make the same sound

as the bell," said the Lemon Boy. "The driver did it just now."

The Lemon Boy looked out from under the front seat. He could see through the front window. He could see shops and offices.

"We are back in the city now," he said to Mouse. "I think we should try and make the driver stop the bus!"

The Lemon Boy said in as loud a voice as he could, "Ting-a-ling."

The driver stopped singing.

"Ting-a-ling," the Lemon Boy said again.

The driver was amazed. Then he felt very worried. He thought the bus was empty. Now he could hear a voice going "ting-a-ling." Maybe the bus was too hot. Maybe he needed fresh air and a cup of tea.

He pulled the bus in at the next bus stop and opened the doors. Mouse and the Lemon Boy rushed out from under the front seat and jumped off the bus onto the pavement. There were people walking along.

Mouse and the Lemon Boy looked around carefully. "Is this our street?" they asked each other. "Which way should we go?"

"Oh, so there you are," said a voice.

Mouse and the Lemon Boy looked up.

Twinkle was flying above their heads. "We were getting very worried. We thought you were lost," Twinkle said.

"We *are* lost!" said Mouse. "Only you can save us."

"No, you are not lost. You are outside the shop," said Twinkle.

Mouse and the Lemon Boy looked at the shop beside them. The window was full of their friends waving at them.

"Well, well," said the Lemon Boy. "We were so worried about being lost that we did not know that we were home."

"Come along inside," said Twinkle

Mouse and the Lemon Boy and Twinkle slipped back in through the letterbox. The Lemon Boy helped Mouse up onto the counter and back into the middle of the window. Then he sat down beside her.

The plastic spider said, "You have been gone a long, long time."

"I know," said Mouse. "But we have had so many adventures."

"Tell us about them," said the spider.

Mouse and the Lemon Boy told their friends all about their adventure in the park with the ducks and the boys on the skate-boards.

Then they told them about their adventures with the horses on the merry-go-round.

Then they told them about their adventure on the fishing boat.

Then they told them about their adventure with the dog near the beach.

Then they told them about the adventure on the bus.

Their friends all said, "Will you teach us the new songs that you heard?"

"We will," said Mouse, "but it might be better if we waited until the night time. People might not like it if they saw us all singing and dancing around the shop."

"That is right," said Twinkle. "We will

sing and dance tonight. Now we should rest."

Everything in the shop window and in the shop rested all day. Then the lights came on outside in the street. Everything was very quiet. All the people had gone home.

Mouse and the Lemon Boy taught their friends all the new songs and dances that they had learned. Everyone had a very good time.

Then it was time to rest again.

"I wonder will Sam and Nan remember to say hello to us in the morning," Mouse said to the Lemon Boy.

"I hope they do," said the Lemon Boy. "I hope too that we will have more adventures soon."

Then Mouse and the Lemon Boy went asleep.

♩♩ Songs ♩♩

♩♩ Words and Music ♩♩

Words by Tony Hickey
Music by Jack Jones

The Song of the Toys

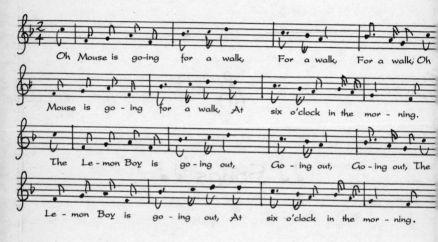

Oh Mouse is go-ing for a walk, For a walk, For a walk, Oh

Mouse is go - ing for a walk, At six o'clock in the mor - ning.

The Le - mon Boy is go - ing out, Go - ing out, Go - ing out, The

Le - mon Boy is go - ing out, At six o'clock in the mor - ning.

The Lemon Boy is going out

Is going out

Is going out

The Lemon Boy is going out

At six o'clock in the morning.

The Song of the Ducks

Wad - dle wad - dle, Quack quack quack, It's so ea - sy
You can do that! Put out your left foot, Then your right,
For - ward step now, Turn to the right, Turn to the right a-gain
Now to the left, Ev'-ry- one to-ge-ther go quack quack quack.

Waddle, waddle,

Quack, quack, quack.

It's so easy

You can do that!

Put out your left foot

Then your right

Forward step now

Turn to the right

Turn to the right again

Now to the left

Everyone together

Go quack, quack, quack.

The Song of the Horses

Here we go round the mer-ry-go-round The merry-go-round The mer-ry-go-round
Here we go round the mer-ry-go-round At eight o' clock in the mor - ning.
Here we go all up in the air All up in the air All up in the air
Then we all go down in the air At eight o' clock in the mor-ning.

Here we go

All up in the air

All up in the air

All up in the air

Then we all go

Down in the air

At eight o'clock in the morning.

The Song of the Seagulls

Seagulls fly high in the sky
High in the sky
High in the sky
Where they eat fresh strawberry pie
And count fish.

Seagulls fly high in the sky
High in the sky
High in the sky
Where they eat fresh baked apple-pie
And count fish.

Seagulls fly high in the sky
High in the sky
High in the sky
Where they eat fresh pineapple pie
And count fish.

Seagulls fly high in the sky
High in the sky
High in the sky
Where they eat fresh raspberry pie
And count fish.

The Song of the Fish

We go swish, We go splash, Un-der the wa-ter, Splash! Splash! Splash!

We swim fast, We swim slow, Where are we go-ing? We don't know.

But we like it, Yes we do, And we hope that you do too.

First we go to the left. Then to the right a-gain, Splash! Splash! Splash!

1

We go swish,
We go splash,
Under the water
Splash! Splash! Splash!

2

We swim fast,
We swim slow,
Where are we going?
We don't know.

3

We like it,
Yes, we do,
And we hope
That you do too.

4

First we go to the left,
Then to the right again,
Splash! Splash! Splash!

The Song of the Dog

Woof! Woof! Woof! My name it is Spot and I've got a lot of bones hid-den in my gar-den.

Woof! Woof! Woof! I bu-ry them here, I bu-ry them there, Oh yes, I've got bones in the gar-den

Woof! Woof! Woof! And if you would like I'll show you just how I Bu-ry my bones in the gar-den.

Woof! Woof! Woof!
My name it is Spot
And I've got a lot
Of bones hidden in the garden.

I bury them here
I bury them there
Oh yes, I've got bones in the garden.

And if you would like
I'll show you just how
I bury my bones in the garden.

The Song of the Bus Driver

I like to drive my bus All a-round the town.
I like the hills that go up And the hills that go down. I
like the streets so full of shops and so crow-ded ev-'ry day But
most of all I love the start of a love-ly sun-ny day.
I love to drive my bus All a-round the town.
I help the peo-ple get on And I help them get down. And
when they want the bus to stop it's a very ea-sy thing For
all they have to do is pull And my bell will ding-a-ling-ling.

I like to drive my bus
All around the town
I like the hills that go up
And the hills that go down.

I like the streets so full of shops
And so crowded every day
But most of all I love the
Start of a lovely sunny day.

I love to drive my bus
All around the town
I help the people get on
And I help them get down.

And when they want the bus to stop
It's a very easy thing
For all they have to do is pull
And my bell will ding-a-ling-ling.